Soapstone Signs

Soapstone Signs

Jeff Pinkney

illustrations by
Darlene Gait

ORCA BOOK PUBLISHERS

Library and Archives Canada Cataloguing in Publication

Pinkney, Jeffrey R. (Jeffrey Richard), 1962-, author
Soapstone signs / Jeff Pinkney ; illustrated by Darlene Gait.
(Orca echoes)

Issued in print and electronic formats.
ISBN 978-1-4598-0400-5 (pbk.).--ISBN 978-1-4598-0401-2 (pdf).--
ISBN 978-1-4598-0402-9 (epub)

I. Gait, Darlene, 1968-, illustrator II. Title. III. Series: Orca echoes
PS8631.I535S62 2014   jc813'.6   c2014-901954-8
c2014-901955-6

First published in the United States, 2014
Library of Congress Control Number: 2014936071

Summary: A young Cree boy learns about soapstone carving from a master carver.

Orca Book Publishers gratefully acknowledges the support for its publishing programs
provided by the following agencies: the Government of Canada through the Canada Book
Fund and the Canada Council for the Arts, and the Province of British Columbia
through the BC Arts Council and the Book Publishing Tax Credit.

*Orca Book Publishers is dedicated to preserving the environment and has printed
this book on Forest Stewardship Council® certified paper.*

Cover artwork and interior illustrations by Darlene Gait
Author photo by Julie Gagné
Illustrator photo by Frances Litman

ORCA BOOK PUBLISHERS   ORCA BOOK PUBLISHERS
PO Box 5626, Stn. B   PO Box 468
Victoria, BC Canada   Custer, WA USA
v8R 6s4   98240-0468

www.orcabook.com
Printed and bound in Canada.

17 16 15 14 • 4 3 2 1

To Mom and Dad, for sending me out in April
and calling me back in September

Soapstone Signs and Whispers:
A Spring Arrival

Lindy travels opposite to the geese. Every spring after the ice breaks up on the river, he walks in from the north along the tracks. Even though his name is Lindbergh, everyone calls him Lindy. Even me. He has a way of being polite without saying anything. He smells like campfires and the outdoors.

Lindy carries a big burlap sack of soapstone pieces. Folks ask where he's found all that soapstone. He just laughs and tells them, "Somewhere between here and there."

Our place is one of the stops on his yearly journey to the south. We operate the lodge between the river and the train tracks. Lindy trades his carving

1

in return for a place to sleep and food to eat. Each year, Mom puts the one he carves for us in the glass display case. Our guests sometimes ask to buy them, but Mom always says, "Not these ones—they are special to us."

When someone asks, "Whatcha working on?" Lindy smiles and says, "Work in progress." He leaves his finished carvings on the ground beside him, and the tourists can look and touch and buy those ones if they want. He carves bears, loons, owls, ospreys, beavers, walrus, seals and even fish.

Lindy has a place he likes to sit by the riverbank. I like to sit with him and watch him carve. Sometimes he hands me what he is working on. I look and then hand it back without saying a word. Really, that is saying a lot.

Today, when Lindy finishes a carving, I become curious. "How do you know what you will carve next?"

He pauses, looking thoughtful. "You ask the stone," he says. "Whatever it is going to be, it is already there."

"How does the stone answer you?"

"Sometimes, you might be given a sign, and then you will know what to carve."

"Do you mean signs like the ones where the train stops?"

"Those are important signs too, but a sign can be any way that the world gives you a message. Signs come to you when your thoughts mix with your senses."

I know what all the senses are. I ask Lindy, "If you mix your thoughts with your sight, can you see what is inside the stone?"

He lifts the piece he is working on, turns his hand and studies it against the clouds. "Sometimes it feels like I can see into the stone."

"Does the stone talk to you?"

"Sometimes I feel like the stone is whispering to me."

"Can you ever tell by the smell and the taste?"

Lindy laughs. "Sometimes the smells and tastes of the world around me give me signs about what is inside the stone."

"Can you tell what is waiting inside by touching the stone?"

"Sometimes if I hold it just so, it's like I can feel what is inside."

"What if the stone won't tell you?"

Lindy reaches into his burlap sack and holds a small piece out to me. "This is for you—ask for yourself."

My very first piece of soapstone. It is dull gray and feels powdery before it is carved. I know from watching Lindy that the soapstone will look different after it is made into a carving. It will polish to a beautiful dark green with black swirls and white shimmers like the northern lights.

I am not sure my ears are sharp enough to hear the soapstone whisper. "Will you tell me what is inside, so I can try to carve it out?"

"That piece of stone has chosen you. Only the one who is to be the carver will know."

"What if it never tells me?"

He laughs again. "Take it with you and be ready for a sign."

I hold the soapstone to my ear all the way home, but it does not speak to me. I ask it lots of questions, but it doesn't reply. I hold it up to a lamp, but I still can't see into it. I cradle the stone until it is as warm as I am, but I still don't know what it's meant to be.

At suppertime, I show off my soapstone and tell everyone about how the carving is already inside it.

"Give it here," my big brother says. "I'll smash it open, and then we'll see what's inside it."

I hold it tightly. After all, it chose me, not him.

I put it under my pillow. I wonder if it will ever speak to me or give me a sign.

That night I dream of the bear cub that comes to the garbage pails out back, and I wake up very excited. I wonder if that counts as a sign.

When I join Lindy on the riverbank, I tell him about my dream. He nods, then hands me a rasp file. "You'd better carve that bear cub out of there."

"Will my signs always come in dreams?" I say.

"Not always, but sometimes."

"Where else will I get my signs?"

"Everywhere, from everything. Stay open to the world around you. You will learn to understand your signs."

I work with Lindy all day. Mom brings us lunch by the riverbank. Tourists come to watch us. Some of them want to know what I am carving, but I just smile and say, "Work in progress."

By suppertime, Lindy has made an owl and a walrus. He has already sold them, plus all the other ones he's made since he arrived at our lodge.

I finally finish my carving. The bear's head is crooked, and its neck too short. I have not left enough stone for one of the ears, and I've forgotten that bear cubs have small tails. I am feeling a bit ashamed of it. Then Lindy takes my stone carving in his hands. "That is a very good bear cub," he says. I start to feel better.

My brother says it looks like roadkill. Dad looks it over carefully, then digs through his toolbox and gives me a rasp file for keeps. Mom asks my permission to put the bear cub in the display case, and I feel very proud.

Lindy stays for as many days as it takes to carve the soapstone pieces in his sack. Mom and Dad always invite him to stay longer, but he never does. Mom packs him some sandwiches. Dad lets me walk him down the tracks to the marker line that tells the train our stop is coming.

At the marker, Lindy stops and shakes my hand like I am a grown-up. He hands me his burlap sack. There are still three nice pieces of soapstone in it.

"I think you are going to be a very good carver," he tells me.

"*Meegwetch*," I say.

"Thank you also," he says.

I watch him disappear to the south. I will practice listening to the stone. I will be ready for the signs. I will wait for the ice to break up on the river and for the geese to fly back home. Most of all, I will watch for Lindy to arrive again. When he does, I will show him my carvings.

Blueberries, Blackflies and Belugas:
A Summer Encounter

I saw *wapamegwak* from the school boat in the last week of school before the summer holiday. I'm sure I did, because sometimes beluga whales swim in from the bay to spend time in the river. But there was just a hint of them way off in the distance toward the bay. "There's the whales!" I yelled. Everyone looked, but no one else saw them. Some big kids said I was only seeing the whitecaps on faraway waves. They asked me on the way home where my "invisible belugas" were.

Lindy uses white stones called gypsum that he's found along the riverbank to carve beluga whales that the tourists love to buy. Except he would say "wapameg," or "wapamegwak" for more than one. That's *beluga* and *whale* in one Cree word.

Every year after the blueberries come out, Mom paddles downriver and camps overnight. She usually goes alone so she can spend some special time remembering. When she gets home, it's blueberry bannock and pies for everyone. This year is different. She has invited me to go with her, and I am excited. I've been camping with the whole family but never just with Mom. We will pick some berries and make a campfire. If I am lucky, maybe I will hear some stories. But I am mostly excited because I know that wapamegwak are out there somewhere.

We make our journey in Mom's canoe. Mom's canoe is made of cedar strips and covered in white canvas. She takes very good care of it.

Mom and I have packed bannock mix, strips of smoked whitefish and some water. We have a first-aid kit, bedrolls and a small tent. She has also packed her rifle in case our camping gets interrupted

by *wapask*, the white bear. I have never seen her take her rifle out of its cover, but Dad once told me she is a better mark than he is and that's one of the reasons he's so good to her.

I have packed one of the soapstone pieces from Lindy. I will be ready to start a new carving as soon as my signs and whispers tell me what is waiting for me inside the stone.

"What if we run out of food?" I ask Mom.

"Then we hunt and we gather. Food is all around us."

"What if the fish won't bite?"

"Then we learn to be hungry—that will make us better hunters."

The blackflies are biting. "I wish there were no bugs!"

"Without the insects, there would be no blueberries or belugas," Mom says. "The insects help turn the blueberry flowers into berries. They also act as food for the fish, and those fish go on to feed the belugas."

"Okay," I say, "but I wish the blackflies would just eat the blueberries instead of biting us."

"Me too," says Mom as she passes me some bug spray.

We paddle out onto the river. With the current flowing toward the bay and the tides pulling in the opposite direction, the river creates tiny "tut-tut" waves. The waves don't go one way or the other but lift straight up into tiny peaks and drop back down again. Little drops are left hanging in the air for a split second. If you listen, it sounds like the gentle *tut-tutting* of a hundred tongues. It's like the river is thinking but can't make up its mind about something.

I have tut-tuts in my ears and blueberries and blackflies in my thoughts. But mostly I'm thinking about belugas and keeping an eye peeled over the water. We are paddling to a place called an estuary, where the salt water of the bay and the fresh water from the rivers inland meet.

There is lots of time to think when you are paddling a canoe.

I think about being a human being, and how when I breathe the air I can feel the breath come in and out of me. I can feel the wind against my body, and I know that it is gravity holding me to the ground. I can see when it is light or dark, and I can feel when it is hot or cold or wet or dry.

Lindy taught me to use my senses to be aware of signs and messages from the world around me. I wonder about the beluga whales who breathe the air like we do, and I wonder about all the signs that they can feel, smell, taste, see and hear in the water.

I think about the fresh water from the river mixing with the salt water in the bay. And I think that must be an important sign for the whales.

I think about how belugas can see, hear, feel, smell and taste just like we can. But they also have

an extra sense that lets them bounce sound through the water around them. This is how they know what else is in the water, like friends, food or danger. I think the belugas must know secrets about the water that people have not thought of yet.

At first, I think we've paddled up beside a long gray river rock. Then I realize that the long gray river rock swam up beside us!

The wapameg is almost as long as our canoe and gently breaks the water beside us. I am tingling with excitement but do not feel scared.

I look up at Mom, who is paddling gently while the whale swims beside us. She motions for me to look across to where a bigger beluga is gliding slowly toward us. This whale is longer and wider, white like snow and floating as gently as a cloud in the sky.

"She is the mother," my mom whispers as the big white wapameg comes slowly alongside. Little Wapameg must have separated and mistook the round white underside of our canoe for the mother's belly.

The small gray wapameg is sounding in trills, squeaks and clicks that we can hear from the water. Mother Wapameg answers in a voice of whistles and calls. It sounds like the little one is asking questions and the mother is patiently answering.

Little Wapameg gets close enough to brush the side of our canoe. Then the whale rolls slightly sideways so that one eye breaks the surface and looks up. Right up at me!

Little Wapameg's eye is big, wet and round. The color is a deep gray, nearly black, shimmering like a mirror and bottomless too. The eye shines like a polished carving stone. I feel Little Wapameg look at me and it's as if we are sharing all the wonder from inside both of us. I feel still and calm.

Mother Wapameg starts to move away from the canoe. She sounds a whistle and makes some clicking noises. Little Wapameg rolls back into the water, clicks in answer and moves slowly forward to catch up. I reach down and touch Little Wapameg on the back—the skin is gray-blue and slippery smooth. The texture makes me imagine how the whale could be cozy and warm inside the cold water.

We can still hear the echoes of the belugas as they slowly move away from the canoe.

Lindy says that whales are magical because you never see them coming—they just appear. Now I know what he means.

"Why do they come here?" I ask Mom. I want to know everything about wapamegwak.

"They like to scratch on the gravelly river bottom while they get ready to molt their old skin. They also like to eat the whitefish that are found here this time of year."

"Is Little Wapameg a new baby?" I whisper.

"No, I have seen them together before. Mother Wapameg has raised a beautiful child."

"Is Little Wapameg a boy or a girl?"

"What do you think?"

"I think Little Wapameg must be a boy."

"I think maybe you are right."

"How will Little Wapameg know when he is all grown up?"

"Little Wapameg is about the same age as you. But what takes wapamegwak one year takes us two. He will turn from gray to white and then will know it is time to swim on his own. Mother Wapameg will soon have to say goodbye."

Mom and I stay floating there until the wapamegwak are out of sight. "We'd better go make camp," Mom says. "We may see them again tomorrow. They will not come to the shallows of the river after the tide is high."

"Why not?" I ask.

"Why do you think?"

I think about that for a whole lot of paddle strokes. "So they don't get stuck when the tide drops?"

"You are getting wise, my son," Mom says. I feel proud to have figured that out.

Soon it will be twilight. We beach our canoe on a gravelly island and pull it up just beyond the high-tide mark. There is a place where fires have been before and a smooth flat spot for the tent.

Mom sets our fire with sticks and dried bark. Out beyond the sedge grass, I can see the bay opening wide and curving with the Earth. Mom says we will stay here until the tide is low and maybe we will see wapamegwak again. While we wait and watch, we will fill our baskets with berries.

I help Mom put the tent up and then pick enough fresh blueberries for the bannock. I gather enough wood to keep a small fire burning all night long and choose some long sticks for the bannock. Mom mixes berries into the batter and packs it onto the ends of the sticks. I set the pail for tea with a few wintergreen leaves for flavor.

I remember the slippery feel of Little Wapameg in the cold river and the warm feeling that went through me when we looked at each other. I make a wish that we can share this river forever. I think of Lindy and then check the soapstone he gave me. I see a beluga whale inside the soapstone, waiting to be carved. Not a big white one and not a baby, but a wapameg who is growing up and getting ready to be on his own.

Powder and Bits:
A Fall Journey

The clay skeets send white dust flying against the blue of the sky. It's like fireworks, but in the daytime. Three in a row fall, powder and bits, onto the snow and mud.

Skeets are like Frisbees made of clay. They get spun into the air and then you shoot them. It's how hunters can practice their aim. My face burns hot and cold all at once, especially the part that presses against the stock. Gunpowder smell is in the air.

The other skeet shooters are making a big deal of my shots. Chief Stan starts calling me Hat-Trick. I swallow a smile way too big for my face because I know those shots weren't just luck.

Dad is looking very proud. My brother is glaring at me, and I can tell he's jealous. He's had his gun for two seasons now, but his skeets still thump to the ground whole.

The fall goose hunt starts after one more sleep, and this time I'm big enough to go. It will be my first time using a shotgun for grown-ups, but I've practiced thousands of times in the bush with a toy one.

I am excited about being part of the fall hunt.

Freighter canoes float against the dark of the early-morning sky. They look black now, but they'll be green in the daylight. People move like shadows as the boats are loaded for the hunt. Stan has invited Dad, me and my brother to join him. We are hunting for the community feast that celebrates the fall harvest.

Stan is Mom's cousin. He is also chief of our band council, and we are very proud of him. He and Dad like to go hunting and fishing together. Lots of people call him Chief, but to my family, he's always just been Stan.

Dad has a big blanket wrapped around my brother and me. We sit on either side of him facing the back bench, where Stan drives the outboard. It is warm beside Dad, and he smells like home. The blanket is cozy, but I am way too excited to sleep.

Spruce, alder and tamarack trees reach from the shadows of shore. They are thin and very old. Stars twinkle through their tops. Behind us, the boat's wake swooshes white against the moonlight, then disappears into the dark purple water.

The tide is out when we arrive at the hunting grounds. The mud sucks hard against our rubber boots as we make our way to shore. I look back at our canoe and know that it will be safe. Anchors are set a special way because of the tides. Our freighter canoe will be bobbing by the grassy shore when we return.

Onshore, there are some fresh patches of snow but mostly sedge grass and hard-packed dirt. Rocks form circles where campfires have been. The charcoal smell hangs in the air when we walk by. The trail to our hunting blind is completely hidden from view, but Stan has walked it many times. He goes right to it.

Dad tells my brother and me to watch the trail. He says we might see footprints from our grandfather's grandfathers. I do not see them, but somehow I can feel them. We walk from the boats to the blind, which is way in on the marshy flatlands. A gentle hand rests on my shoulder. I look up and Stan is smiling at me.

"Hi, Stan," I say.

Stan has a way of being silent.

"What if the geese don't come this morning?" I ask him.

"Then we go to plan B."

"What's plan B?"

"Kentucky Fried Chicken."

"Okay, Stan." We both start to laugh.

He slaps me on the back like I've seen him do to Dad. When I look back down to my shotgun, I feel taller.

The blind is like a little tent made of tree branches and covered in dried grasses. Built to hide hunters from the geese, it is open at the top for shooting. All four of us fit inside, but just barely. Decoy geese made of tamarack are set up in front of the blind. One of the hunters will make noises like a goose. Real geese are tricked by the decoys into flying down to have some food.

Time passes in a special way when you are hunting. No one speaks and we hardly move. We all just sit and watch the sky turn from purple to light blue. Stan gives the signal and then shoulders his gun. We have agreed that he will shoot first.

Dad's call sounds just like a snow goose. It was the birds that brought him here, but Mom who made

him want to stay. At least, that's what he tells almost every guest who comes to our lodge. He doesn't get to shoot, because hunting season for white folks starts later in the fall. White folks also have to be sixteen to start hunting, so Dad says the Cree side of me better do the hunting for a few years.

Geese appear like specks against the morning sky. Then wings, bodies and necks start to take shape. One swoops down, and Stan does not miss. Three more times he does not miss.

My brother and I are sent to collect the downed geese. We have to be fast and quiet. The geese are big, heavy and still warm as we try to gather them in our arms. Some blood trickles down my arm as I hurry back, and I have to look away.

Next, my brother takes his turn. Dad calls and a goose comes circling down. My brother shoots—but too soon. The bird ruffles its feathers and swoops back up and out of sight.

"We'll try again," Stan whispers.

On his second try, my brother misses again. He wants one so bad. He glares at me like he wishes I had a beak and feathers. Then, on his third try, he brings one down. My brother whoops so loud that Dad has to shush him, but the tension is gone and everyone is happy in the blind.

My turn comes, and I shoulder my gun. I hear Dad call. A far-off answer comes from the sky, and a speck turns to wings circling downward. I trace the bird and wait. The shot feels sure, just like the skeets did yesterday. I have butterflies in my stomach, but it's as if they are flying in formation.

I watch the beautiful snow goose, thinking about its long journey across the world and back again. If I went all the way across the world, I would long to come home as well. I think about how it's just seeking food and safety before winter comes. And I think about how in springtime, when the snow goose flies back home, it will be a sign that Lindy will soon be here.

Something in me moves the gun barrel as I squeeze the trigger. The goose shifts in the air and flies up and away. I look behind me to where Stan is sitting. His face is lined up along my gun barrel, his head slightly tilted. His eyes meet mine in a questioning way. He knows I missed on purpose. I look away quickly. After that I reload, and Dad continues to make his calls. No more geese come down, which means the hunt is over for the day.

We return from the hunt. There will be no need to order fried chicken for tomorrow's community feast.

The next evening, geese and bannock cook slowly on sticks that lean over large fires. The air smells delicious and is full of laughter. Everyone is happy. It's the kind of happiness you feel when you have saved up your hunger on purpose.

On winter hunting grounds, the hunters eat first and the elders eat last, in case there is not enough food. At community feasts, the elders eat first and then the children. The hunters and cooks who provided the feast eat last. Everyone eats as much as they want.

The elders are served, and the children are called to line up for food. I start toward the line and feel a familiar hand, strong but gentle, on my shoulder. It is Chief Stan, wearing his eagle feather. He says that I will be served with the hunters today.

"Okay, Stan," I say—but my voice is very small. I have not looked him in the eye since the hunt.

I stand with my dad, brother and all the other hunters while people line up to fill their plates. We stand proudly. Stan motions for me to be the first hunter to go to the serving tables, and the community claps and cheers. I have so many feelings fighting inside me that I do not want to look up. I do not feel very hungry.

One of the soapstone pieces that Lindy gave me is in my pocket, along with my rasp file. He won't be back until spring, but I have been wishing he was here. I want to ask him about when my signs and whispers tell me to do opposite things. After the feast I will walk down to the riverbank, where I can be by myself and begin to carve. Inside the stone, there is a snow goose in flight.

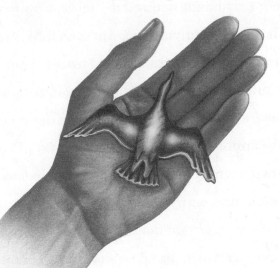

River Weasels:
A Winter Discovery

So far I have carved a bear cub, a beluga whale and a snow goose, and I am getting better at it. I have one more piece to carve before spring, when Lindy comes back to visit my family. I am excited to show him my carvings. I am open to signs so I can learn what is waiting for me inside the very last piece of soapstone.

Right now it is wintertime. We have lots of wintertime where I live. The ice on the river gets thick enough to skate on safely. Sometimes the wind clears off the snow and we can skate for just about forever. And around here, if it's winter, it's also hockey season.

Mom is a hockey nut, and she comes out to practice with us. She has this move she calls the "ol' dipsy-doodle," where she pretends to pass but keeps the puck on her stick. She laughs every time she does it, and when we get tricked, we laugh too. But I am getting wise to it and even try it on my brother sometimes.

My brother and I play in the kids' league at the arena on Saturday mornings. This is our first year. We are rookies together.

Between shifts on the ice, the players sit on a long bench. Everyone comes in one door, sits on the bench and slides down toward the other door. That's how you know it's getting close to your turn on the ice again.

My brother and I stick together so we can be on the ice at the same time. We are almost the whole way down the bench when these two other bigger brothers come and push us. Then they take our turns. Some other kids on the bench laugh, and one says that river weasels like us don't belong there.

The coach doesn't notice right away. Then we get our turns again. My brother is so upset that he smashes his stick on the ice, and he gets put in the penalty box for doing it. When I am back on the bench without him, the same kids tease me, saying, "Aww, do you miss your big brother?"

I do miss him. But I will not show it. I try not to let the teasing take all the fun out of the hockey. I am learning that not all signs feel good—some are signs of danger.

We still have our hockey stuff on when we Ski-Doo home, so we head right out onto the river rink for more. We pass the puck back and forth. I'm not sure if I want to go back to the arena. I think my brother feels the same way, because his passes are too hard and he keeps staring down at the ice. Trouble is, I really like hockey. And my brother is getting really good at it.

Mom and Dad are out skating with us. Dad has a stick, and he gets the puck and carries it way down the ice. We race after him in a mad scramble. Dad fires the puck and it goes whipping around the bend of the shore and out of sight.

We hustle around the bend and then come to a screeching halt. A romp of otters has made a slide on the snowy riverbank. When they see us come around the corner, they stop and look startled, just like we did. Then they start right back up with their fun.

The otters slide on their bellies, head first with their legs tucked under their bodies. They go whooshing out onto the ice, where they roll and wrestle. Their squeaky chitter-chatter noises sound like laughter. When they stop, they untangle themselves and race back up the bank.

Mom and Dad catch up to us and watch. Even when you're sad, it's hard to watch otters and not smile and laugh along. There are four of them in their family too.

The otters push their way into a spot near the bottom of the snow slide and disappear under the ice. I guess it must be their suppertime, like it is for us.

My brother and I skate up closer to where the otters were. There is a mess of crayfish shells on the ice and lots of otter footprints. There's also an icy line down the snow hill that their bodies made when sliding.

Our hockey puck is nowhere to be found.

At dinner, we talk about the otters and the teasing.

Mom tells us that the thing she likes most about otters is that they see all other living creatures as likeable and friendly. She says an otter will never be the first to start a fight and only fights back if really pushed. Some might think this is a sign of weakness, but Mom says it's a sign of real smarts.

When it is Saturday again, Mom and Dad take us back to hockey. I'm kind of scared but keep the otters' example in my heart.

When my brother and I are out on the ice together, I stop a shot that is getting close to our own goalie. We both start skating as fast as we can toward the other team's net. We even get to do the passing-back-and-forth thing Mom taught us—but in the real arena! We get all the way to the other team's blue line, and a defense player skates toward me. I decide I'll try the "ol' dipsy-doodle" trick on him. I pretend to pass but keep the puck and deke past him. I pass it over to where I know my brother is going to be. He takes the pass and tries a snap shot, and it flies right over the stretched-out goalie and gets mesh! We put our sticks in the air, then tear off to the bench. All the hands are out for high fives, even the teasers!

After the game, we head back to our river rink. We still haven't had enough hockey. My brother can't stop smiling. It's another one of those days where you can skate forever. Mom and Dad join us, and we all decide to go check on the romp of otters. We find the spot, but they are not out playing today.

We do find something though. Right at the spot where the otters swooshed out onto the ice, we find the missing puck from last week. My brother picks it up and tosses it to me. I put it in my pocket.

I am ready to start carving the last piece of soapstone that Lindy gave me. My signs have shown me that there is a river otter inside. Tonight when I am warm by the fire, I will begin. My otter will be sliding on the hockey puck, having fun. But he will have a brave face too.

Acknowledgments

The author offers his special thanks to editor Amy Collins for patiently refining and polishing the story, to Greg Spence for advising on usage of Moose Factory Cree (or the L dialect), to Joanne Findon and Orm Mitchell, who taught the writing classes at Trent U where it all began, to a wonderful network of friends and family who helped guide the story and its route to publication, and to Darlene Gait, for capturing such magic in her incredible illustrations.

Jeff Pinkney holds an English degree from Trent University, is a former newspaper columnist, and currently works as a business advisor. *Soapstone Signs*, his first work of fiction, draws on Jeff's experiences while traveling as a development consultant in Canada's James Bay Frontier, where he acquired a deep appreciation for the people and the landscape. Jeff is an emerging poet, writer and an amateur stone carver. He and his wife Leslie share a brood of three story-loving daughters. They are surrounded by soapstone carvings in their Peterborough, Ontario home. Learn more at www.jeffpinkney.com.

Darlene Gait is a Native American artist from the Coast Salish Esquimalt Nation. Her work captivates Native and non-Native people alike through its expression of unity between people and with nature. Known for her work on Victoria's Unity Wall, her coin designs for the Royal Canadian Mint, and her art gallery, One Moon Gallery, Darlene continues to inspire, create and take her work in many different directions. She currently resides in Victoria, British Columbia.

Orca Echoes

Orca Echoes

Orca Echoes

Orca Echoes

Visit www.orcabook.com for all our titles.